Splish, Splat!

WRITTEN BY ALEXIS DOMNEY
ILLUSTRATED BY ALICE CRAWFORD

Produced in partnership with the
Canadian Cultural Society of the Deaf

Second Story Press

1
3
2

Colin had his own bedroom. It was a very nice room, but there was one problem. The walls were a hideous yellow. Colin felt like he was sleeping in an egg yolk! It was giving him nightmares.

Colin's mom, Betty, told him he could have his room painted. And just to make sure it was all done perfectly, she decided to hire real painters to do the job. She called a painting company.

The man on the phone gave her two phone numbers and told her to call the message relay number first. Message relay? Betty was confused. "The painters I am recommending are Deaf," said the man. "Put the call through message relay and then ask for Heather."

Betty followed the instructions and soon made an appointment with Heather.

The next day, two painters came to the house. They introduced themselves.

"Hi," signed Heather. She pulled out her notebook and wrote: "I'm Heather and she's Molly."

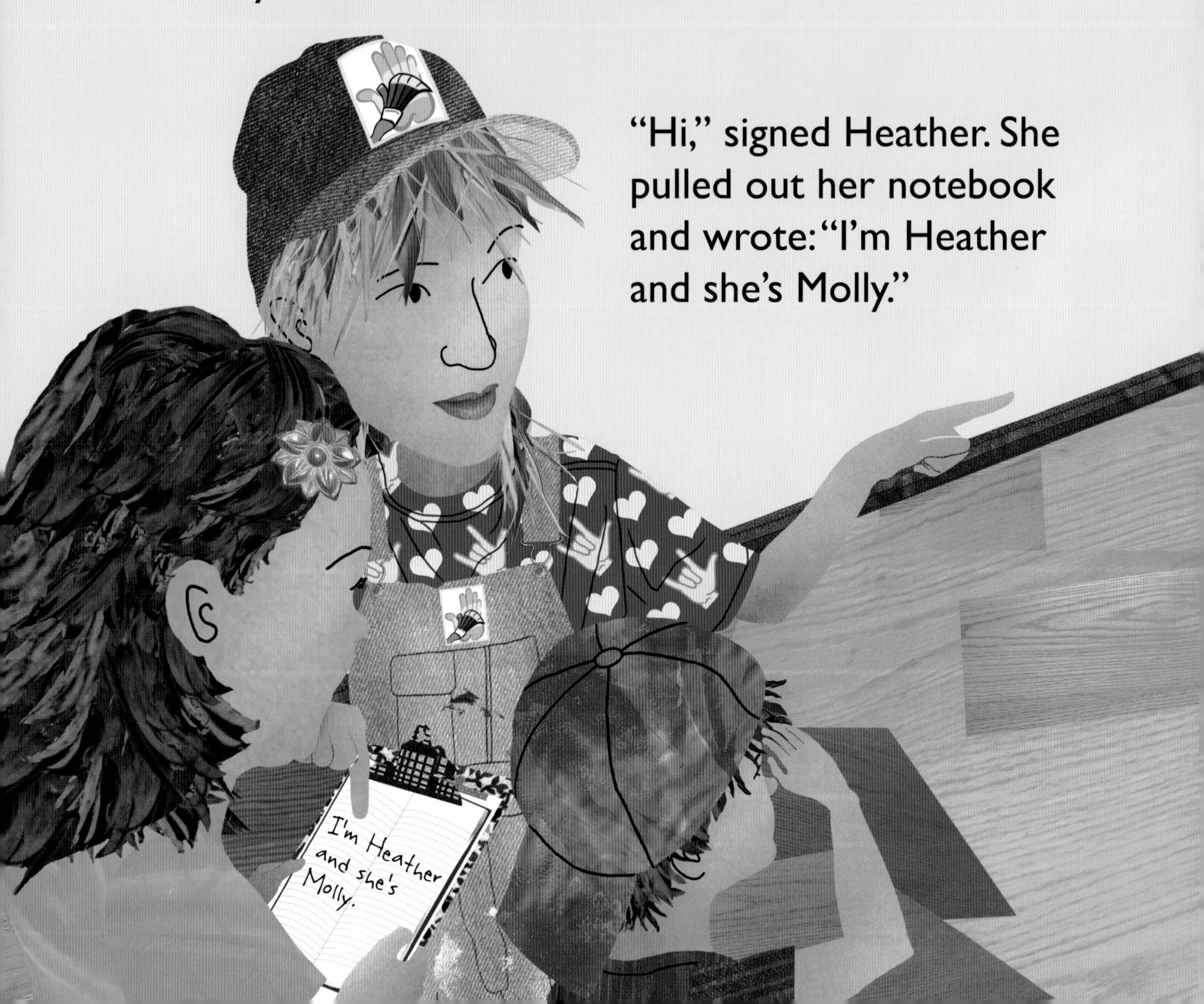

Then she pointed to each of them. "You're Betty, right? And this must be Colin."

Betty and Colin nodded and took the women upstairs to see Colin's yellow nightmare.

Colin and Betty had already been thinking of colors. They had sample paint chips taped to one of the yellow walls. Colin looked at the painters and said, "I want navy blue."

Betty, gesturing and pointing, added, "And please do the trim and ceiling in white. That would look nice."

Heather watched her face and gestures and wrote, "No problem. We'll go and get the paint and start right away."

509

They were back in a flash and started to unload their van. Colin watched them bring in ladders and brushes and rollers and big sheets of plastic to protect the floors and furniture. "This could be fun," he thought.

Betty could read Colin's mind. "You come with me, young man," she said, steering Colin into the kitchen so the painters could get to work.

Molly and Heather started to paint — first the white ceiling and then the navy blue walls.

It was looking good, they thought, but it was getting late. Luckily, there was just the white trim left to do and then no more egg yolk! They'd be finished.

Heather and Molly dipped their brushes in the white paint. Splish, splat! They painted and chatted and chatted and painted furiously.

When they were done, they put away their tools and rushed downstairs to tell Betty and Colin they were finished.

Everyone ran back upstairs to see the room.

509

Betty's mouth fell open.

Heather covered her face with her hands.

Molly turned fire-engine red.

Colin just stared and stared.

The walls were navy blue all right — but there were white splish-splats all over them!

"What happened?" Betty asked, gesturing.

The painters looked at each other. "We were chatting, signing with our brushes in our hands, and I guess the paint flew off and splotched the walls," Heather wrote.

She looked very upset and was about to write more, when Colin stepped into the middle of the room, threw his arms up in the air and yelled, "Wait! This is *my* room, and I *like* it!! No more nightmares for me. This is a room I can dream in!"

Everyone started to grin. And while Betty paid Heather and Molly a heap of dollars for the creative job they had done, Colin ran out to tell his friends about his polka-dot dream room and his new friends, the painters.

Some of the ASL signs used in the book

meet

near

thank you

you

Fingerspelling Alphabet

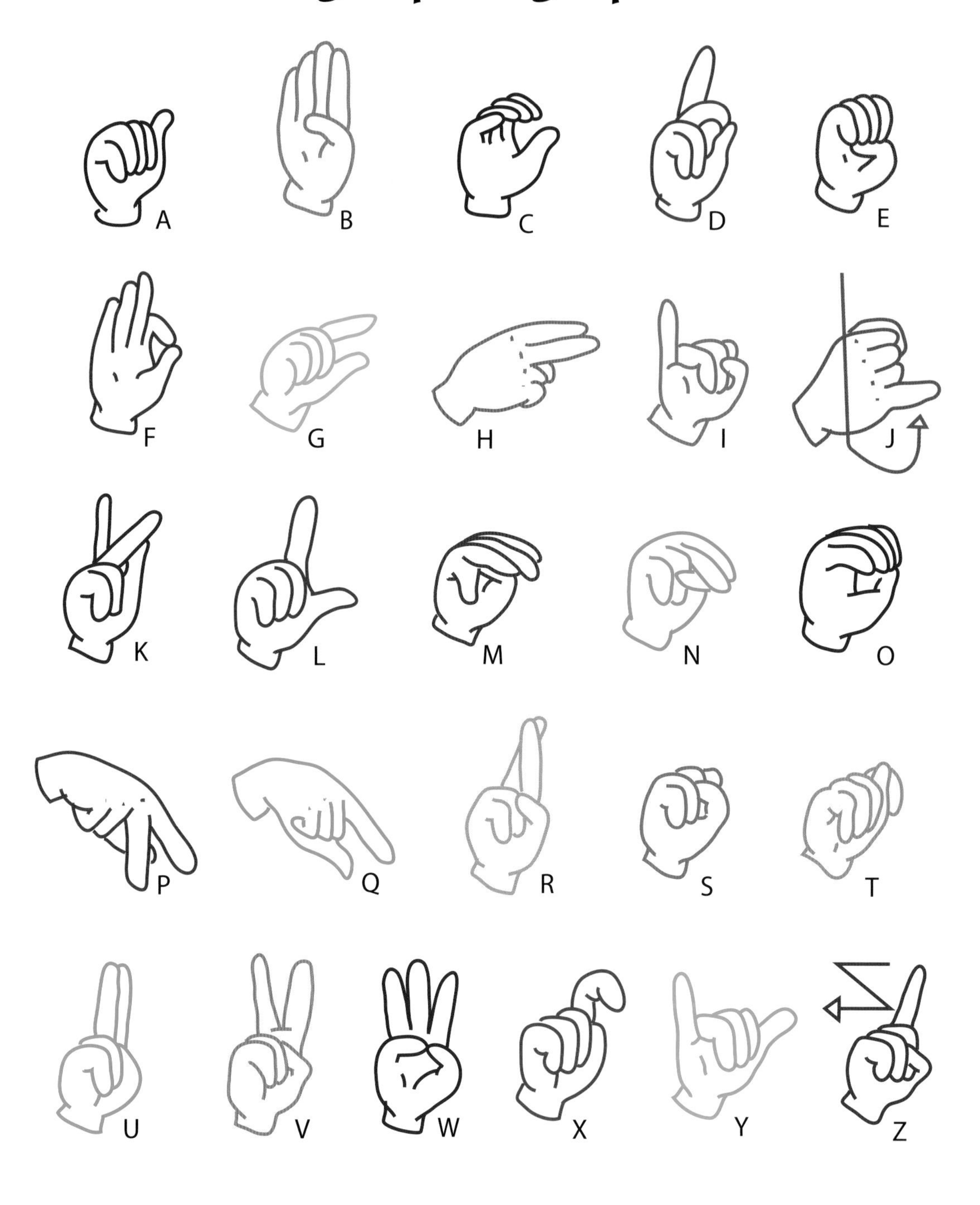

Library and Archives Canada Cataloguing in Publication

Domney, Alexis, 1985-
Splish, splat! / written by Alexis Domney ;
illustrated by Alice Crawford.

Published with the Canadian Cultural Society of the Deaf.

ISBN 978-1-897187-88-3

I. Crawford, Alice, 1954-
II. Canadian Cultural Society of the Deaf III. Title.

PS8607.O495S75 2011   jC813'.6   C2011-900362-7

Alice Crawford's website: www.papercut-design.com
Fingerspelling alphabet designed by Jeri Alice Cripps

The Canadian Cultural Society of the Deaf website:
www.deafculturecentre.ca

Second Story Press gratefully acknowledges the support of the Ontario Arts Council and the Canada Council for the Arts for our publishing program. We acknowledge the financial support of the Government of Canada through the Book Publishing Industry Development Program.

Printed and bound in China

Canada Council for the Arts
Conseil des Arts du Canada

Published by
Second Story Press
20 Maud Street, Suite 401
Toronto, Ontario, Canada
M5V 2M5
www.secondstorypress.ca